The
Straight
Line
Wonder

For Michael Beresford-Plummer—M.F.

To Willy, an appreciator of lines—M.R.

The illustrations were rendered in India ink and watercolor.

This edition first published in the United States of America
in 1997 by MONDO Publishing
By arrangement with MULTIMEDIA INTERNATIONAL (UK) LTD

Text copyright © 1997, 1987 by Mem Fox
Illustrations copyright © 1997 by Marc Rosenthal

For information contact:
MONDO Publishing
One Plaza Road
Greenvale, New York 11548

Printed in Hong Kong by South China Printing Co. (1988) Ltd.
First Mondo printing, October 1996

96 97 98 99 00 01   9 8 7 6 5 4 3 2 1

Text originally published in Australia in 1987 by Horwitz Publications Pty Ltd
Original development by Robert Andersen & Associates and Snowball Educational

Designed by Becky Terhune
Production by Our House

Library of Congress Cataloging-in-Publication Data
Fox, Mem, 1946-
The straight line wonder / by Mem Fox ; illustrated by Marc Rosenthal.
p.   cm.
Summary: Despite the admonitions of his friends, a straight line enjoys
expressing himself by twirling in whirls, pointing his joints, and creeping in heaps.
ISBN 1-57255-206-9. — ISBN 1-57255-205-0 (pbk.)
(1. Individuality—Fiction. 2. Self-realization—Fiction.) I. Rosenthal, Marc,
1949- ill. II. Title.
PZ7.F8373St   1996
(E)—dc20   96-3708
CIP
AC

The Straight Line Wonder

by Mem Fox

pictures by
Marc Rosenthal

Once upon a time there were three straight lines. They were the best of friends.

One day the first straight line said, "I'm tired of being straight all the time," and he began to jump in humps.

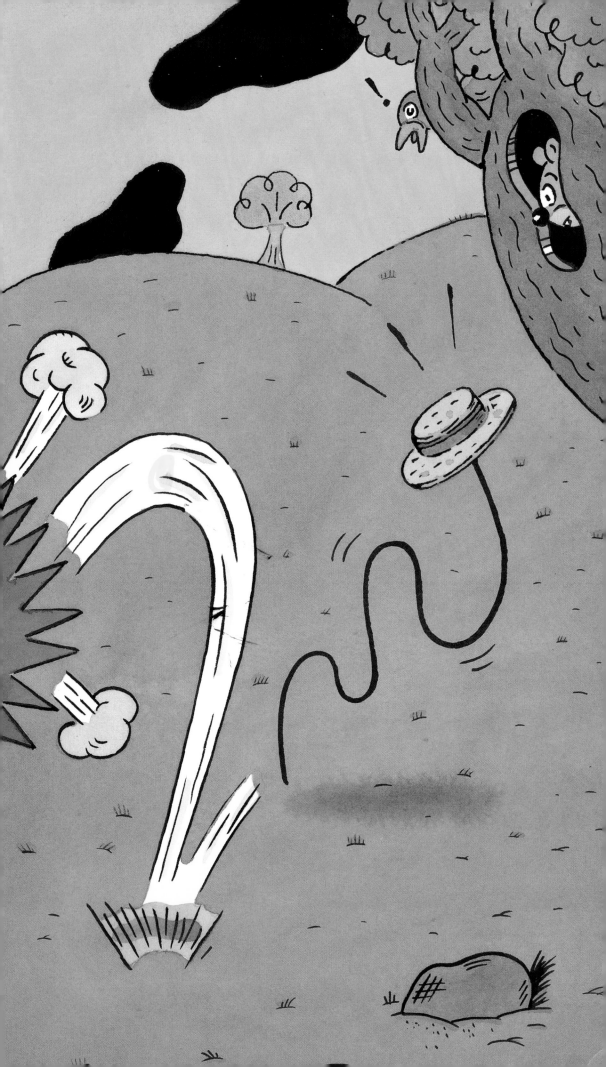

"Stay straight, silly!"

said the second straight line.

"People will stare!"

said the third straight line.
"I don't mind," said the first straight line, and he kept on jumping in humps.

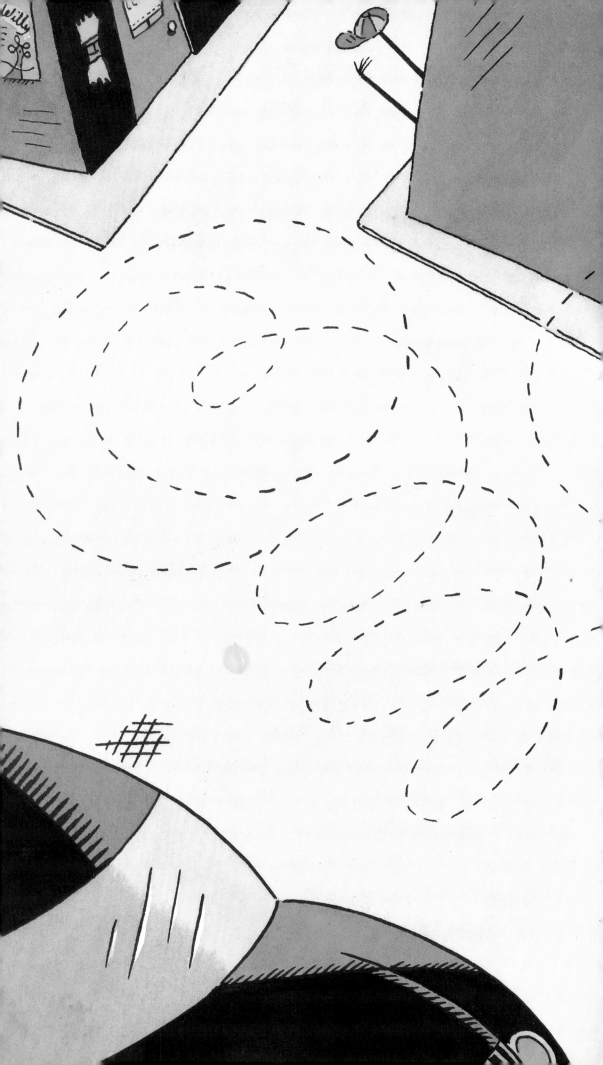

Next day, the first straight line began to twirl in whirls.

"Stay straight, silly!" said the second straight line.

"People will stare!" said the third straight line.

"I don't mind," said the first straight line, and he kept on jumping in humps and twirling in whirls.

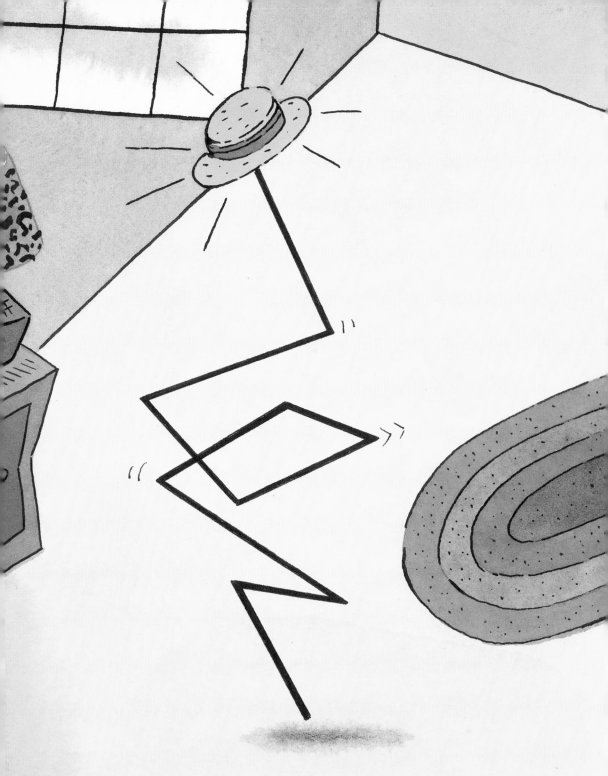

A few days later the first straight line
began to point his joints.

"Stay straight, silly!" said the second straight line.

"People will stare!" said the third straight line.

"I don't mind," said the first straight line, and he kept on jumping in humps, twirling in whirls, and pointing his joints

Not long after that the first straight
line began to creep in heaps.

"Stay straight, silly!" said the second
straight line.

"People will stare!" said the third
straight line.

"I don't mind," said the first straight line, and he kept on jumping in humps, twirling in whirls, pointing his joints, and creeping in heaps.

the Maginot Line

Finally, the first straight line began to spring in rings.

"Stay straight, silly!" said the second straight line.

"People will stare!" said the third straight line.

and
springing
in rings.

creeping
in heaps,

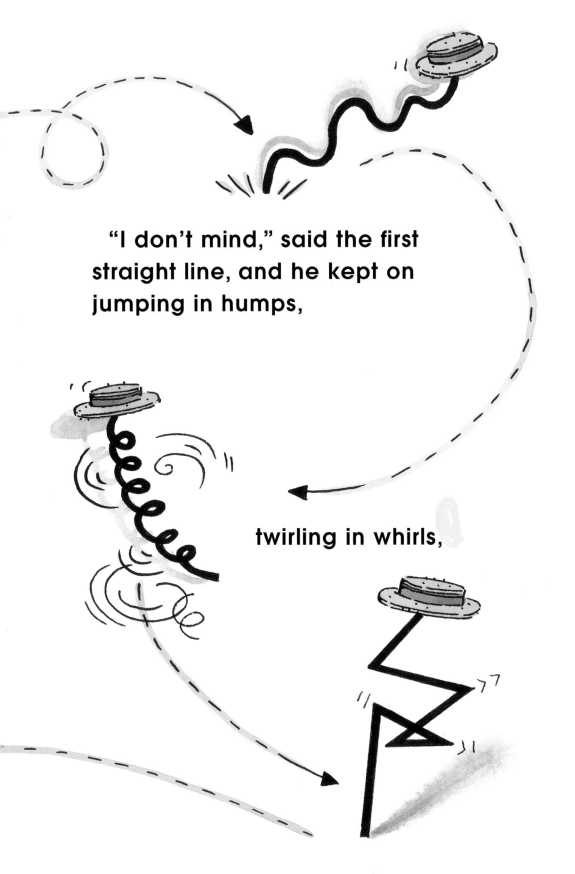

"I don't mind," said the first straight line, and he kept on jumping in humps,

twirling in whirls,

pointing his joints,

"Stop that this minute!"

yelled the other straight lines. "You're supposed to be a *straight* line, remember?"

And they ran off and left him.

One day a famous film director happened to see the first straight line jumping in humps, twirling in whirls, pointing his joints, creeping in heaps, and springing in rings, one after the other and then all together.

Club
La Ligne

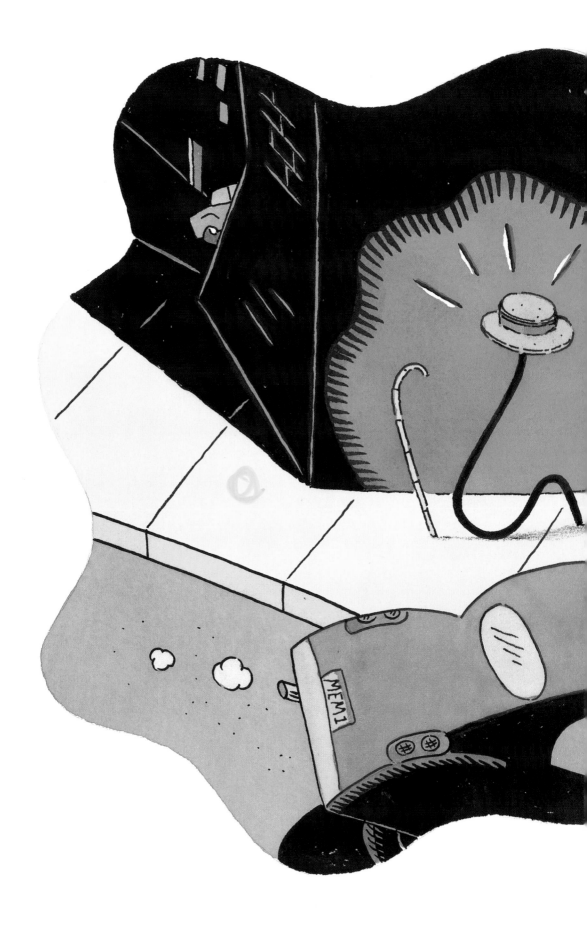

"You're a wonder!"

said the famous film director.

"I just love the way you move.

Come and be the star in my
latest movie!"

And so it was that the first straight
line grew up to be a great star.
Now he jumps in humps every day

and twirls in whirls and points
his joints and creeps in heaps
and springs in rings.

He dances entranced
and pauses for applause
and bows to the crowds
who throw flowers for hours
because they love him so much.

The other straight lines are pleased to know him.

"He's my friend," says the second straight line.

"He's my best friend," says the third straight line.

And the first straight line is tremendously happy because he never has to be a straight line again.